East Africa
Bush
rhinoceros
golden pipit
impala
ostrich
praying mantis
milky eagle owl
tuxalis grasshopper
lesser kudu
silk moth caterpillar
chameleon
spider
dik-dik
guinea fowl
leopard
giraffe

Desert
dwarf hedgehog
five-lined skink
desert lark
viper
agama agama lizard
gerbil
beisa oryx
kori bustard

Swamp
didric cuckoo
marsh owl
herald snake
marsh mongoose
bohor reedbuck
little bittern
water lily frog
lesser swamp warbler
purple heron
Nile crocodile
soft-shelled turtle
sitatunga

We Hide, You Seek

by Jose Aruego and Ariane Dewey

MULBERRY BOOKS • New York

For Juan

Published by Greenwillow Books, a Division of William Morrow & Company, Inc., 105 Madison Avenue, New York, N.Y. 10016
First Mulberry Edition, 1988 Printed in the United States of America 1 2 3 4 5 6 7 8 9 10

Library of Congress Cataloging in Publication Data Aruego, Jose. We hide, you seek.
Summary: The reader is invited to find animals hidden in their natural habitat. [1. Hide-and-seek—Fiction.
2. Camouflage (Biology)—Fiction. 3. Animals—Habitations—Fiction] I. Dewey, Ariane, joint author.
II. Title. PZ7.A5227 We [E] 78-13638 ISBN 0-688-07815-X

Let's play.
We hide
and you seek.

We'll play too.

Ready or not, here I come!

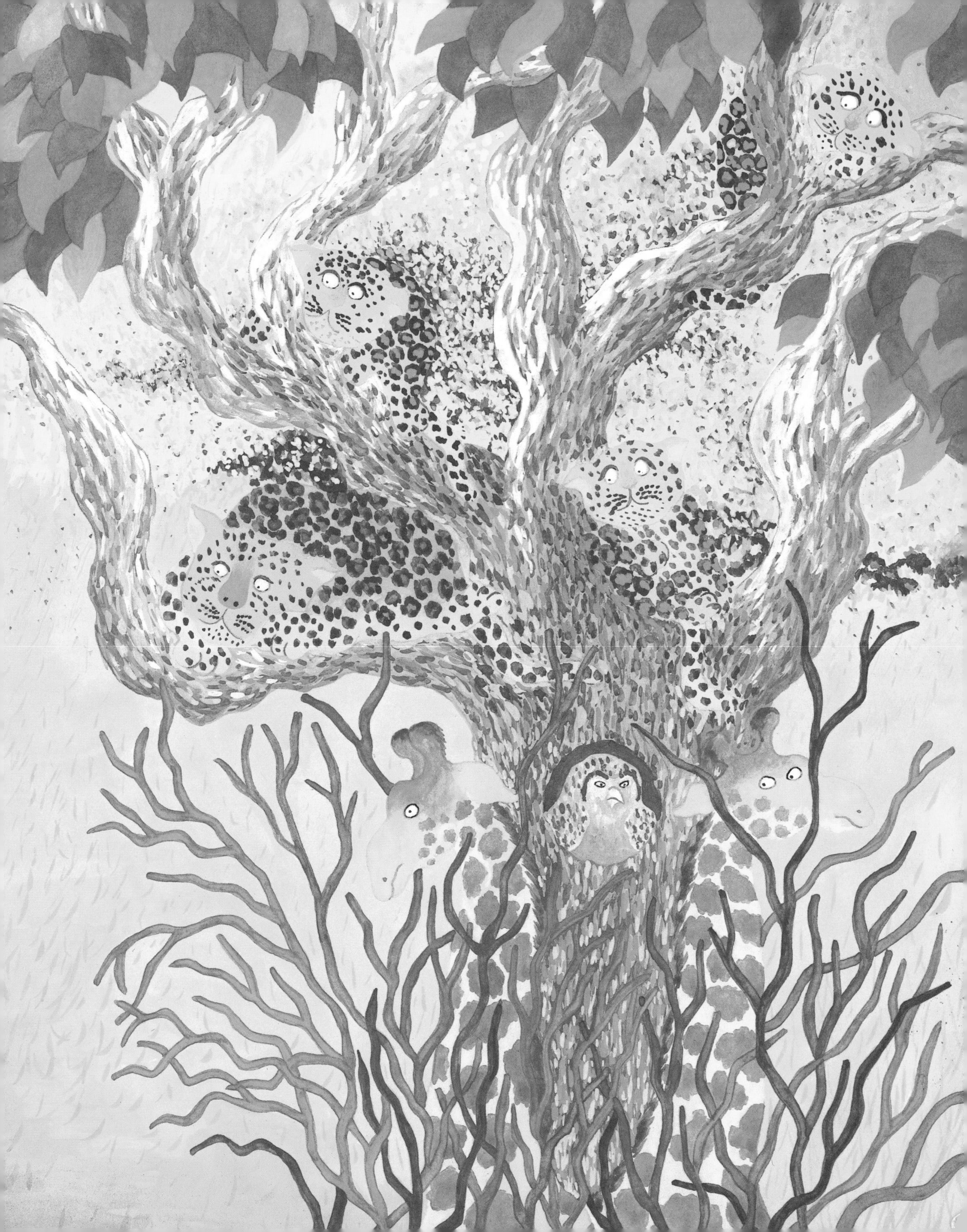

Now I want my turn to hide.

Where are you?

Plains
dusky nightjar
button quail
kongoni
silver-backed jackal
spotted hyena
zebra
scops owl
pectoral-patch cisticola
ostrich
cheetah
lion
wildebeest
rosy-breasted longclaw

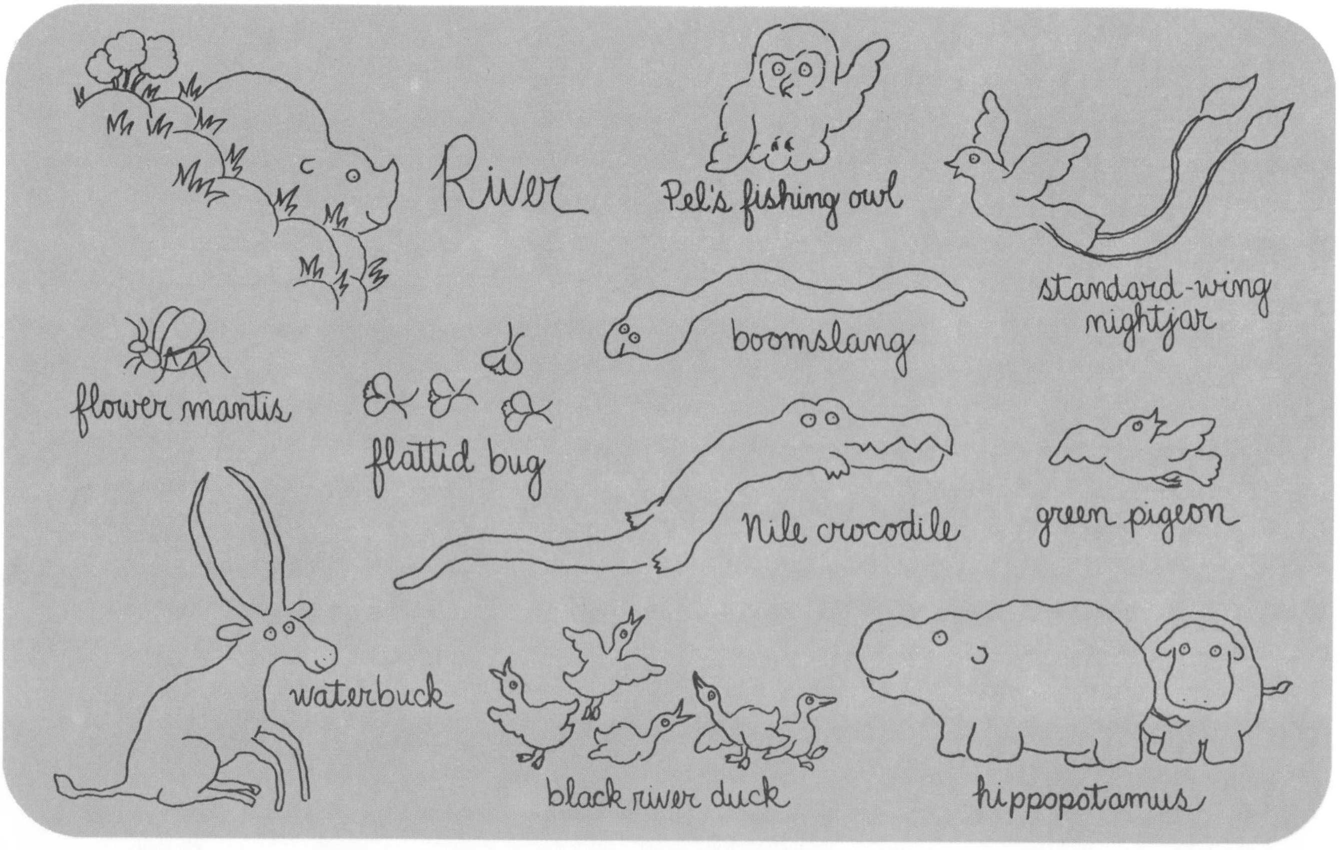
River
Pel's fishing owl
standard-wing nightjar
boomslang
flower mantis
flattid bug
Nile crocodile
green pigeon
waterbuck
black river duck
hippopotamus